Quest for
Columbus

Quest for Columbus

by **L. A. Peacock**
illustrated by **Nathan Hale**

Scholastic Inc.
New York Toronto London Auckland
Sydney Mexico City New Delhi Hong Kong

For Jen and Lia Fine Rotti,
two little girls who like big books — *L.A.F.*

ISBN 978-0-545-46043-9

12 11 10 9 8 7 6 5 4 3 2 1   12 13 14 15 16 17/0

Printed in the U.S.A.   40

First Scholastic printing, September 2012

Chapter 1

The Lost Letter

"Hey, Josh!" yelled Jess. "You awake?"

There was something on her desk. It was large and round. Jess leaned over to get a better look.

"Josh, hurry!" she called again. "You have to see *this*!"

Jess was dressed in her pink pajamas. They were covered with white bunnies. Her furry slippers looked like bunnies, too.

Josh turned on the light. It was after midnight. He had been sound asleep.

"Oh, man," he said, rubbing his eyes.

Josh pulled on his slippers and rushed to Jess's room. It was dark, except for the desk

lamp and the bright screen of the Wizard.

"Strange," Jess mumbled. She typed some words into the Wizard. Josh's twin sister liked to look up facts in the Wizard's encyclopedia.

"What's up?" he said, standing at the door. The light of the desk lamp shone on a large globe of the world.

Jess pressed the Wizard's Search key.

"Take a look," she said, pointing to the globe.

Josh walked over. His gaze fell on the globe. Close up, he could see that it was old. It was cracked, too.

Jess twirled the ancient globe.

"Where did you get it?" asked Josh.

"In the attic," she said, "behind Uncle Harry's trunk." Their uncle was an explorer and time traveler. When Uncle Harry needed help, he left a mysterious time-compass in his trunk. The magic device took the twins to places in the past.

Josh stared at the globe. *Was this a clue about their next adventure?*

"Well," said Jess. She crossed her arms. "See anything strange?" A thin smile was on her face.

Josh reached out and made the globe stop. Sometimes his sister could be a pain. She was smart and liked to show off.

He turned the globe slowly and looked closer. Something was wrong.

"Oh, brother," said Josh. The names were hard to read.

"Latin?" said Josh, looking up in surprise. He knew the ancient language from their time travels to Roman times and Pompeii.

"What else?" said Jess.

Josh studied the map again. He pointed to the biggest land area. "I see Russia and India, so this part must be Asia."

Jess nodded.

Next, Josh moved his finger across the globe. "This must be Europe," he said. Then he moved his finger down. "And Africa." A lot of the names were funny.

"Turn the globe around," said Jess. "What do you see *now*?"

"Huh?" said Josh. He was back to Asia! "Cathay" was marked. It was the old name for China.

Josh kept on turning the globe, shaking his head. Something BIG was missing. *Where were North and South America?*

He looked up. "There's nothing else," he said. "Just more ocean."

"Exactly," said Jess, picking up the Wizard. She read aloud.

○ WIZARD

In the 1400s, people in Europe knew about Asia, Europe, and Africa. Explorers had traveled eastward over land to India, Japan, and China. It took years to reach these places, called the Indies, and bring back spices and gold to Europe.

Josh had an idea. He spun the globe again. This time, toward the *west*.

"If people from Europe traveled the *other* way, across the ocean," said Josh, "they could get to the Indies faster!"

"Yes," said Jess. "If you believed the world was round . . ."

". . . and you didn't know about North and South America," Josh added.

Jess clicked to the next screen.

The Italian explorer Christopher Columbus believed the Earth was round. He had a plan to find a western sea route to the Indies. He showed the Spanish King Ferdinand and Queen Isabella a map of the world he made himself.

"Yeah," said Josh. "We studied Columbus in school. Didn't he promise to bring back gold from China if the queen paid for his trip?"

"Right," said Jess. "There's more."

> ∘ Wizard
>
> In 1492, Columbus set sail with three ships—the *Niña*, the *Pinta*, and the *Santa Maria*—from Palos, Spain. First, he sailed to the Canary Islands off the coast of Africa to pick up supplies.

Jess turned off the Wizard and put it in her pocket. She stood up.

"We're going to the attic," she said.

Josh nodded. "I'll get the flashlight."

Minutes later, they were climbing the ladder to the attic. Uncle Harry's trunk was in the corner.

Josh held the flashlight while Jess searched the trunk.

"It's here," said Jess. She wrapped her hand around Uncle Harry's journal. The time-compass was there, too, in Uncle Harry's leather bag.

"Hold this," said Jess, tossing the bag to Josh. She sat on the floor and flipped through the journal. The pages were filled with drawings and notes in Uncle Harry's tiny handwriting.

Jess looked for clues.

Josh crouched down next to her. He turned the light on the last entry. It was new.

"Uncle Harry drew a map," said Jess, "of Columbus's voyage."

"The Canary Islands," whispered Josh, "and September 6, 1492!" They had a place and a time in the past to set the time-compass.

Jess looked at Josh. "What's in Uncle Harry's bag?"

Josh reached in the bag and took out the

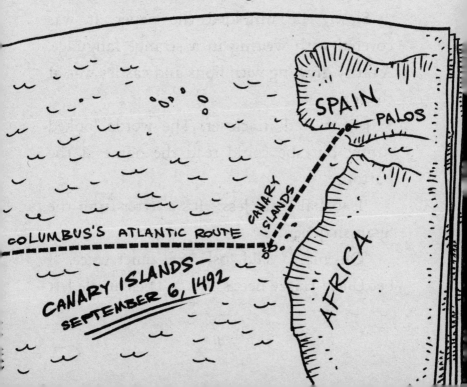

COLUMBUS'S ATLANTIC ROUTE

SPAIN

PALOS

CANARY ISLANDS

AFRICA

CANARY ISLANDS—
SEPTEMBER 6, 1492

time-compass. He didn't see the paper in the corner.

"Anything else?" asked Jess. Uncle Harry hid things in his bag. The twins helped him return these lost objects to their real owners.

Josh flipped over the bag. Something fell out.

"What's that?" asked Jess. She pointed to the yellow paper on the floor.

"I'm not sure," said Josh, "but it looks old."

Slowly, he unfolded the paper. It was covered with writing in a strange language. A fancy drawing with lions and castles was at the top.

Jess moved in closer. The words looked funny, but she could read the name at the bottom.

"Isabella!" said Jess. "It's a letter from the Spanish queen."

"Oh, man!" said Josh in a quiet voice. "I bet Uncle Harry needs this." Their uncle left

important objects in the trunk to keep them safe.

Carefully, Josh folded the letter and tucked it back into the leather bag.

Jess nodded. It was time to find their uncle and return the letter to Columbus.

Quickly, Josh pulled out the time-compass and moved the hands into position.

He threw the leather bag over his shoulder and wrapped his fingers around the time-compass. It was set for the Canary Islands, September 6, 1492.

Josh turned to Jess. "Ready?"

Jess patted her pocket. The Wizard was there.

The time-compass made loud clicking noises.

Josh grabbed his sister's hand. The room began to spin.

A flash of light filled the attic.

Then everything was quiet.

Chapter 2
Three Tall Ships

Jess felt the hot sun on her face and smelled the salt air. She heard the waves as they hit against the dock.

"Wow," said Jess. She looked down. Magically, her pajamas were gone. She was wearing a cotton shirt and brown pants. A bandanna was around her neck.

She wiggled her toes and giggled.

Josh was barefoot, too. He wore a shirt and pants, just like hers.

Josh took a long look at Jess.

"Wait!" he said. He pulled a wool cap from his pocket. "Put this on," said Josh, handing the cap to his sister.

Jess made a face. "What for?" she argued. But she pushed her long hair into the cap.

"It's scratchy!" she complained.

"Now you look like a boy," he said. "Nobody will notice you now, *Jessie*."

"*Jessie*, huh?" she said. Jess had a new name, a boy's name.

"Look," said Josh. He pointed to three tall ships in the harbor. "They look like pirate ships."

Jess shook her head. "They aren't pirate ships. See the flags on top?" she said. "They show a castle and a lion, not a skull and bones."

Josh nodded.

"Yeah, the Spanish flag," he said, "just like the drawing on Isabella's letter."

Jess raced along the dock and stopped.

Shading her eyes from the sun, Jess gazed at the three ships with the Spanish flags. Men were climbing the ropes and opening the sails. Others were on deck, cleaning the cannons.

She counted more than thirty sailors on the biggest ship.

"Come on!" she called back.

Josh caught up to her. He was close enough to read the names of the ships.

"*Niña, Pinta, . . .*" he read aloud.

". . . and the *Santa Maria*," said Jess.

They had found Columbus's ships. But where was Uncle Harry?

Suddenly, they heard a loud voice.

"Grab that rope!" shouted one of the sailors.

Josh turned. The language was strange, but Josh understood. It was the magic of the time-compass.

"Need help?" Jess answered in the strange new language. She kept her voice low, like a boy's.

Josh looked around. Wooden crates were stacked along the dock. They were ready to be loaded onto the ships.

The rope was swinging toward Jess. At the end was a metal hook.

Jess reached up to grab the rope.

"Wait," called another voice from behind. A boy stepped forward and pulled in the rope. He held the hook in his hand and attached the rope to a large crate. Then he tugged.

Suddenly, the crate next to Jess started to move. The boy shoved it loose, while Josh

pushed. The rope went stiff. The huge crate rose in the air. It swung up over the dock onto the deck of the ship.

"Hello," said Josh, turning to the boy. "My name is Josh, and that's my . . . uh . . . brother, Jessie." He remembered the new name just in time.

Jess held out her hand. "Jessie, that's my name." She sounded like a boy.

"I'm Pedro." The boy smiled. "That's the *Santa Maria*." He pointed to the largest ship.

They watched as a tall man stepped onto the deck. He wore a velvet cape. A cap with a long feather covered most of his red hair. His arms were filled with maps and charts.

"That's Captain Columbus," said Pedro. "He is taking us to the Indies. The captain says there is much gold there."

Jess and Josh looked at each other. *Pedro did not know about the New World!*

Just then, they heard a shout.

"Pedro!" yelled one of the sailors. "Catch the rope!"

Pedro glanced up. "I have to go," he said. "The crates must be loaded before sunset."

He ran to the end of the dock and turned.

"We sail tonight with the tide!" he called.

Josh and Jess looked at each other.

"Oh, no," cried Jess. "We'll never find Uncle Harry now!"

Josh stared at the crates stacked next to them. With a smile on his face, he looked up at Jess.

"Wait," she said. "I know that look."

Josh knelt down next to a large crate. He saw a stick and stuck it under the lid.

Jess shook her head. "Are you nuts?"

Josh grinned as he pushed hard against the stick. Finally, the crate opened. Josh pulled back the top.

On her toes, Jess peered into the wooden box.

"Oranges?" she asked in surprise.

"Yep," said Josh. "Vitamin C. If sailors don't eat oranges on long trips, their teeth can fall out."

He put one leg over the side of the crate.

"Once I'm inside," said Josh, "you come after me."

He pushed aside some of the fruit and dove in.

Jess took a deep breath and jumped into the crate.

"Whoa!" she said, falling on a pile of oranges.

"Shh!" said Josh.

Quickly, he pushed the lid back over their heads.

Chapter 3

Stowaways

Jess peered out through the cracks of the crate. Pedro was coming toward them with the rope. Her heart pounded as he attached the hook.

"Hang on!" Jess whispered. Josh pushed against the sides of the crate to keep his balance.

The twins were hidden in the box of oranges.

"Take her up!" shouted Pedro, tugging on the rope. In a few seconds, the wooden box was swinging in the air above the ship.

With a thud, the crate hit the deck.

"Give me a hand," yelled a sailor in a gruff voice. "Boy, these oranges are heavy." Two men ran over and dragged the crate across the deck of the *Santa Maria*. They lifted the box into the ship's cargo hold.

Jess and Josh held their breath.

The men stacked the crate below deck. Nobody noticed the stowaways.

It took the rest of the day to load the supplies. By sunset, all sailors were on deck. They were getting ready to sail.

Deep in the cargo hold, it was cold and dark. Waves splashed against the sides of the ship. The *Santa Maria* pulled away from port with the tide. Its large square sails picked up the wind, carrying the ship westward.

"Whoa," moaned Jess, leaning against the corner of the crate. She rolled a few oranges out of the way.

"Josh," she whispered. "Are you all right?"

"I'm okay, I guess," he answered, rubbing his head. Josh felt around in the darkness for Uncle Harry's bag.

"Found it!" he said with a sigh of relief. He clutched the leather bag to his side. The letter from Queen Isabella was safe inside.

Jess reached into her pocket and pulled out the Wizard. She moved next to Josh and turned it on. The bright screen lit up the inside of the crate.

"Type in 'Canary Islands,'" said Josh, "and 'Christopher Columbus.'"

Jess clicked on Search and read:

```
o Wizard

Columbus sailed westward from
the Canary Islands. The trade
winds, blowing from east to
west, carried his ships across
the ocean. He calculated 3,000
miles, or about a month of sailing
west, to reach Asia.
```

Josh shook his head.

"Boy," he said, "was Columbus wrong."

"Yeah," said Jess. "Columbus didn't know about North America."

She clicked to the next screen.

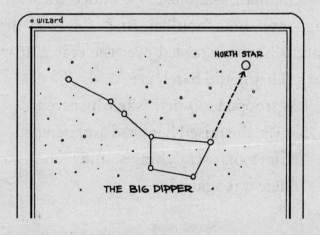

> ○ Wizard
>
> Columbus was a skilled
> navigator. For direction,
> he used a compass. To find
> latitude—where the ship was
> north or south of the equator—he
> measured the angle between the
> horizon and the North Star.

Jess looked up. "The Big Dipper!" she said. "That's how you find the North Star."

She typed more words into the Wizard.

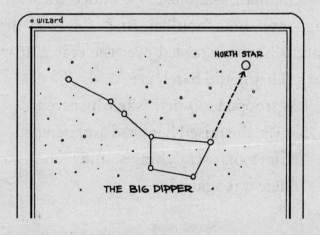

THE BIG DIPPER

"There," said Jess, "the North Star." She pointed to the bright star above the Big Dipper.

Jess turned off the Wizard and stood up. With a quick push, she lifted the top of the crate and jumped over the side.

"Hey," said Josh. "Where are you going?"

"Come on," called Jess, waving to her brother. "I bet we can see the North Star from the deck!"

She headed toward the open hatch. Light from the full moon showed a narrow set of stairs leading up.

"Oh, man," said Josh. He pulled the leather bag over his shoulder and followed Jess. Carefully, they crawled over the crates. It was dark. They could barely see.

Jess stopped. "Quiet!" she whispered.

Slowly, she raised her head and listened.

"What's that scratching sound?" she asked.

"There it is again."

Josh heard it, too. He glanced around the ship's cargo hold. Pairs of tiny yellow eyes peeked from behind the crates.

Just then, a small furry body scurried across their path.

"Rats!" said Josh. "Lots of them."

Jess let out a long breath.

"Hurry," she said, crawling as fast as she could. Jess reached the narrow stairs.

"Careful," said Josh. He was right behind her.

Jess nodded. She took a step up. And slipped.

"Whoops!" said Jess. She fell backward against Josh.

"Watch out!" he warned, holding her steady. The stairs were old.

They started up again. With each step, the wooden stairs made a creaking sound.

That worried Josh. He hoped all the sailors were asleep.

Finally, they stood on the top step.

Moonlight poured onto the deck. Everything was quiet.

Together, Josh and Jess peeked out the hatch.

Slowly, they climbed out.

"Gotcha!" boomed a deep voice from above.

Chapter 4

Under the Stars

"Well, well," said the sailor. "What do we have here?"

A bald man with a bushy black beard peered down at them. There were tattoos on his hairy arms.

Jess shuddered. His large hands were on her shoulders. She couldn't move.

Another man grabbed Josh. His crooked smile showed missing teeth. The sailor held Josh's arms behind his back.

"Let him go!" yelled Jess, kicking her captor in the shins.

The bald sailor tightened his grip. He threw

his head back and laughed. Grabbing Jess's shirt, he lifted her in the air.

"Put me down!" shouted Jess. She kicked wildly, but the seamen only cheered louder.

"Stowaways," said the bald man, tossing Jess onto the deck. He turned toward the other sailors.

"Maybe we should throw them overboard?" His laugh was loud and ugly.

"No!" shouted Josh. He made fists with his hands. With a shove, Josh broke free and ran over to Jess.

He had to think.

"We're *not* stowaways!" he shouted, pushing Jess to the side.

The sailors formed a circle around the twins.

"What exactly *are* we?" Jess whispered. She pulled the woolen cap tighter on her head and moved behind Josh.

Josh stood tall to protect his sister.

"What do we do now?" asked Jess in a quiet voice. The men were way too close. She could hear their growls and smell their bad breath.

Josh shrugged.

Suddenly, everyone looked up. A tall man walked onto the deck. There were mumbles of "Aye, Captain" as the sailors stepped aside.

Christopher Columbus stood in front of Jess and Josh.

"Who are you?" he asked.

Jess stepped forward. "I'm Jessie," she said in a deep voice. "And this is my brother, Josh."

Josh nodded. His eyes met the captain's.

"We came to help you," he said.

"We're sailors, too," said Jess. She folded her arms across her chest and stood up straight.

Jess gazed at the night sky. Quickly, she found the Big Dipper and pointed to the bright star just above it.

"That's the North Star," she said with confidence.

The captain turned and followed her gaze.

"Indeed, it is," he said, and smiled. His blue eyes twinkled.

Josh looked up. He pointed to the thick ropes hanging from the main mast. It was a long way to the top.

"I can climb up there," he said.

"Please, sir," said a young voice from behind the captain. Pedro moved to the front of the crowd.

Josh and Jess recognized their friend from the dock.

Pedro stood next to Josh.

"We can use another lookout, captain," said Pedro. He turned to Josh and Jess. "I know these boys," he said. "They will work hard."

The bald sailor agreed. "Aye, Captain," he said. "The youngest boys are the fastest on the high ropes."

The captain nodded.

"We will see," he said.

Columbus turned to Jess.

"Be on the poop deck," he said, "for the next watch."

Jess followed his gaze to the high deck at the back of the ship. A large sandglass was hanging on a rope. It was where Columbus navigated the ship.

The captain spoke to the bald sailor.

"Luis," he ordered. "Show the other lad his duties. He can help Pedro with the lookout."

Jess and Josh let out a sigh of relief.

With a nod to the crew, Columbus made his way to his cabin below. The crowd broke up.

"Come on!" Luis led Jess and Josh across the large open deck. He tossed them some scratchy woolen blankets.

"There." Luis pointed to a space against the forward mast. Jess looked around. Sailors were rolled in their blankets, snoring loudly.

Josh spread out the blankets.

Luis leaned over Jess. His ugly face was close. She could smell his bad breath.

"Get up at three o'clock," said Luis in a gruff voice. Then he turned and walked away.

Jess shuddered. She wrapped the blanket tight around her.

Pedro sat beside them.

"Luis was in jail," said Pedro, "but the captain needed sailors. Luis will be a free man when we get to the Indies."

Jess couldn't believe it.

"Prisoners," she said in a quiet voice. Now she was *really* scared!

Jess peered into the darkness. The night air was cool.

"Food," said Pedro. He handed them hard biscuits and flasks of water. First he dunked the cracker in his water jar. Then he took a bite.

"We get hot food in the morning," said Pedro. He pulled his blanket over his head and went to sleep.

Josh stared at the hard cracker in his hand.

"Looks like a dog biscuit," said Jess, putting hers aside. She used her blanket to cover the Wizard. She showed the screen to Josh.

Hardtack is made from flour, water, and salt. It lasts for a long time, so it is good food for long sea voyages. Sailors hold it over fire to drive out the weevils.

"*Weevils?*" asked Jess.

"Bugs," said Josh.

She gave him a funny look.

Josh was hungry. He didn't see any weevils, so he dunked the hardtack in water, let it get soft, and ate.

"Not bad," said Josh, wiping the crumbs from his shirt.

"I'll wait for breakfast," said Jess, shaking her head. Her brother was definitely nuts.

She squeezed her eyes shut and fell asleep.

Chapter 5

Lessons at Sea

The sound of a bell woke them up. It was three o'clock in the morning.

Stars sparkled in the sky above. There was a gentle wind. The swells of the ocean pushed the ship forward.

"Hurry," said Pedro. The twins jumped up. They swayed as they got their sea legs. Around them, sailors were putting away their bedrolls.

Jess and Josh had the early watch, from three to seven in the morning. The crew worked in four-hour shifts.

Josh yawned. "Oh, man," he said, stretching his back. It was the middle of the night!

Jess pulled the cap tight over her long

hair. She looked around. *Uncle Harry must be somewhere on this ship*, she thought.

Pedro turned to Josh.

"Race you!" Pedro ran ahead to the tallest mast and started to climb.

"Whoopie!" yelled Josh, grabbing one of the thick ropes. He pulled himself up the riggings beneath the sails.

"Hey!" yelled Jess. "Be careful!" Both boys were climbing quickly and swinging from the ropes.

At the top of the main mast was a small platform. Pedro was the first to reach the crow's nest. Josh was right behind him.

Jess shook her head. Josh was always doing crazy things.

Just then, Jess felt a heavy hand on her shoulder.

She looked up into the mean face of the bald sailor.

"Let me go!" she yelled, and pushed Luis away.

The big man frowned.

Jess faced the bully. She tried to look brave.

"Go on, boy," said Luis finally. He pointed toward the back of the boat. Up ahead, Columbus was waiting on the poop deck.

Jess ran across the deck and stood in front of the captain.

"Ready for your lesson in navigation?" he asked. A compass was on a table next to a chart and logbook. Sand was flowing slowly in the hourglass.

Jess nodded.

"Find the North Star," ordered Columbus. In his hands, he held a measuring device. It was circle-shaped and made of metal.

The night sky was clear. Moonlight sparkled over the water. Jess raised her arm and pointed to the bright star above the Big Dipper.

Columbus smiled. "Now, point your other arm to where the sea meets the sky. That's the horizon."

Jess had both arms stretched. Her arms made an angle.

"The angle between your arms measures our latitude, the distance we are from the equator," said the captain.

Jess knew when one arm was straight up and the other arm was straight to the side, the angle was ninety degrees. Half of that was forty-five degrees.

Jess looked at her arms. The angle was less than that, maybe half of forty-five degrees.

She glanced at the compass on the table. The needle was pointing north.

Columbus was waiting for her reply.

She guessed. "So we're about twenty-two degrees north?"

"Good," he said, raising the circular device. "This is an astrolabe. It measures latitude." He pointed it to the North Star. Turning the dial, he found the horizon. Columbus made a mark on the chart to show the position of the ship.

"Twenty-three degrees north latitude," he said. "Every four hours, we plot our course. Time, direction, and speed. Where we are on our voyage."

Jess reached for the sandglass.

"What's this for?" she asked

Columbus showed Jess how to measure time. When all the sand flowed from the top half to the bottom half, Jess turned the glass.

This happened every half hour. Each time, she made a mark in the logbook.

Across the open sea, Jess could see the *Niña* and *Pinta* in the moonlight. They were the smaller ships in Columbus's fleet.

Maybe Uncle Harry is on one of those ships? Jess wondered. So far, they had not seen their uncle on board the *Santa Maria*.

Time passed quickly during the watch.

Columbus was an experienced navigator. He leaned over the side of the ship. He could see the whitecaps of the waves and guess how fast the ship was going.

Every time Jess turned the hourglass, Columbus checked his charts.

At the end of the watch, the captain gave a new direction to keep the *Santa Maria* on course.

Below the poop deck was the helmsman. His job was to hold the tiller and steer the ship.

Columbus walked over to the hatch leading to the deck below. He called out his order to the helmsman.

Jess stared at the opening. She watched the captain shout the new course.

Finally, a reply boomed from below. "Aye, aye, captain!"

Jess gasped. She knew that voice.

"Uncle Harry!" she whispered as the ship turned in the new direction.

Chapter 6
Trouble on Deck

"I heard his voice," said Jess. "I *know* it was Uncle Harry!"

Josh grabbed a wooden bowl.

The twins were in line with the other seamen. Time for a hot breakfast.

Josh and Jess were headed for the iron stove on the far deck. It was an open firebox. A big pot was cooking on the wood fire. Buckets of water were nearby in case of fire.

"Are you sure?" asked Josh. He handed a bowl to Jess.

Jess nodded. "I know that voice. It was him. Uncle Harry *is* the helmsman."

"Oh, brother," said Josh. He pulled the

leather bag across his back. Queen Isabella's letter was inside.

They reached the big stove. Pedro was there.

"The *fogón*," said Pedro. "That's what we call the firebox."

He crouched down and put more wood into the stove. Flames leaped around the new logs. On top, the pot was boiling over.

The fishy smell from the pot was strong.

Josh gave him his bowl.

Jess groaned. "I changed my mind," she said. "I'm not hungry." But her stomach growled.

"Come on, Jessie," said Josh. "Just try it."

Slowly, Jess held out her bowl. "Okay," she said. "But just a little."

Pedro tilted the heavy pot and poured the thick soup.

"Fish stew," he said. He handed them two spoons and some hardtack.

The twins found places to sit against the railing.

"Not bad," said Jess. The stew was hot and tasted good.

Josh licked the last drop on his spoon.

More sailors were getting breakfast.

"Maybe we'll be lucky," said Jess. "Uncle Harry might come up for breakfast." She searched the faces of the sailors.

Suddenly, she saw him at the end of the line.

"There," said Jess, elbowing Josh.

Josh followed Jess's gaze to the tall sailor with the ponytail. Their eyes met. Their uncle raised his finger. "Shh!" he signaled.

Uncle Harry filled his bowl at the fogón. Then he walked over and sat down between the twins. Nobody noticed.

Jess and Josh leaned in.

"Awesome!" said their uncle.

"Oh, boy," whispered Josh. "Are we happy to see *you*!"

Uncle Harry pulled them closer into a big hug. "My brave Jess and Josh!"

"Jessie!" she corrected, using her boy's voice. Jess pulled her cap lower.

Uncle Harry laughed.

"We followed the clues in the journal," she said in a rush. "And Josh set the time-compass."

Josh opened the leather bag and started to pull out the folded paper. "And we have the letter from Queen Isabella!"

Their uncle reached out and put his hand over Josh's.

"Not here," he said. The deck was filled with seamen.

He was silent for a time. Thinking.

Uncle Harry turned to Josh and Jess. "Go to Columbus's cabin. Can you find his logbook? That's where the letter belongs."

"I know it," said Jess. "The book has a brown cover. Every day, the captain writes down how far we sail."

Jess jumped up.

"Wait," said their uncle. He stared at the fogón. Flames were leaping around the large pot. An accident at the iron stove could easily start a fire.

"I'll start a small fire," he said. "Everyone will try to put it out. You find the logbook."

The twins nodded.

"Let's go!" cried Uncle Harry. They all got up.

Nobody was looking. Uncle Harry walked across the deck. He raised his foot and kicked a burning log. Flames leaped around the firebox.

"Fire! Fire!" yelled a sailor.

"Get water!" shouted another sailor. Everyone on deck grabbed buckets of water. The fire was spreading. It would take a while to put out the flames.

Jess and Josh raced toward the captain's cabin. They hurried down the stairs, closing the wooden door behind them.

The room was empty.

On top of the large table in the corner was the brown book.

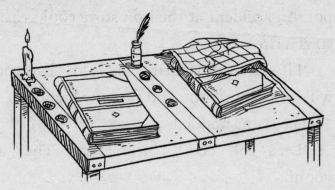

"I've got it," said Jess. In her arms, she held the logbook.

Josh moved aside some charts. He picked up another book. It had a brown cover, too. Just like Jess's book.

"Huh?" whispered Josh. "*Two* logbooks?"

Chapter 7
At Sea

Jess stared at the book in Josh's hands.

"Strange," she said. She looked confused.

They put the two books side by side. Together, they compared books. Page by page, the logbooks were the same. Only the measurements were different.

"Look here," said Jess, pointing to some numbers. "The miles that we sailed each day are different."

"Yeah," said Josh. "My book shows *more* miles."

He looked puzzled. "Why keep different records? Why two logbooks?"

Jess pulled out the Wizard and searched:

> Columbus kept two logbooks.
> One was a false log. Crossing
> the ocean might take a long time.
> The sailors might worry if the
> voyage was too long.

"I hear the sailors complain all the time," said Josh.

"Me, too," said Jess. "Some sailors think the earth is flat."

"Yeah," said Josh. "They think the ship will fall off the edge of the ocean. They want Columbus to turn around and go home."

Jess clicked to the next page.

> Columbus recorded *fewer* miles
> in the false logbook. That's the
> one he showed the crew. They
> would think that they were closer
> to Spain and feel safe.

"Oh, man," said Josh. "It's a trick."

Just then, the bell sounded. Loud voices and heavy footsteps came from the deck above.

Jess looked up.

"Hurry," she said. "Time for the next watch."

Josh opened the logbook in his hand. It was the *real* book. He stuffed Isabella's letter under the cover.

Quickly, they put both books back and left the cabin.

The days passed slowly. Four hours of work, four hours of rest. Life on the *Santa Maria* fell into an easy routine.

It was the tenth day at sea.

"Did you see the comet, Uncle Harry?" asked Jess, getting in line for breakfast.

"No," said their uncle. "I was below deck last night."

"But it was so close!" said Jess. "I saw the comet's tail fall into the sea." She had been on the poop deck when the comet crossed the sky.

Just then, Luis stepped behind them. He stared at Jess and frowned.

"The comet could have hit the ship," said the big man, shaking his head. "It's bad luck." Luis was superstitious. Most sailors were.

Other sailors joined in.

"It's a curse," said an old seaman. "I never saw one so close."

"Aye," two others agreed.

More sailors grumbled.

"We should turn around and go home," said the old seaman. The voyage was much longer than the crew had expected.

Jess shrugged. She knew the charts. They would not see land for *three* weeks!

Trouble was ahead.

The wind picked up the next day. It pushed the small fleet in a different direction.

Josh and Pedro were on the ropes, hanging off the main mast.

"Hey," shouted Josh, pointing to a large patch of bright green seaweed. "What's that?"

Pedro climbed higher. The *Santa Maria* sailed forward into more and more weeds. It looked like a river of tall grass in the middle of the ocean.

Jess leaned over the rail. "Look!" she yelled. "Small crabs are crawling over the reeds, hundreds of them!"

"Maybe it's a sign of land," said Pedro.

Jess ducked behind the mast and pulled out the Wizard. With a few quick strokes, she found the answer:

o Wizard

The Sargasso Sea

Columbus discovered this mass of floating weed in the North Atlantic Ocean. This bright seaweed gets its name from the Portuguese word for gulfweed.

"No," she cried, shaking her head. "It's just very green sea grass."

More sailors were leaning over. Luis pointed to the weeds.

"A sure sign of land," he said. The others agreed.

"Keep your eyes open, Pedro!" shouted Luis.

"Look!" Josh waved toward the side of the ship.

All heads turned.

Dolphins were leaping up and down in the water.

The sailors nodded. It was an omen.

Maybe their luck was changing.

Chapter 8

The Storm

There was no land in sight. For days, the three ships drifted in the sea of weeds. The crew grumbled. They blamed Columbus for the bad luck.

More days passed. At last, the ships pulled free of the weeds. Overhead, dark clouds gathered. From the southwest, a headwind rose up. High waves pounded against the ship.

They were in a bad storm.

Uncle Harry was at the tiller below deck. He held the ship on course against the heavy winds.

Rain swept across the *Santa Maria*. The crew fought to pull in the sails. Barrels were rolling across the deck. The sailors tied them down, too.

"Pedro! Jessie!" shouted Luis, pointing. "Grab that rope." With his strong shoulders, he pushed the fogón against the railing and held it there.

Ten-foot waves crashed on the deck. The ship swayed back and forth on the high seas.

"Come on," called Jess. Holding tight to Pedro, she looped the rope around her shoulder. Step by step, they made their way across the slippery deck.

Luis stretched his arm and caught Pedro's hand. He pulled the kids against him.

"The rope!" shouted Luis. "Wrap it around the iron stove."

Quickly, Jess grabbed the rope from her shoulder.

"The other side!" she cried, waving to Pedro to go around her.

She held the end of the rope while Pedro looped it around the fogón.

Luis turned to Jess. They were eye-to-eye.

"Good work, boy," he muttered. There was a grin on his face as he hurried to tie the knots.

Jess nodded. Maybe the big man wasn't so bad after all.

Just then, a big wave crashed. Water poured in over the rails.

Jess slipped on the wet deck. When she tried to stand up, water filled her nose. The wave had knocked Pedro over, too.

Before another wave hit the ship, Pedro got to his feet.

Everything was happening fast.

"Over here!" shouted Jess, coughing loudly. She raised her head, only to fall backward. The wind was blowing hard.

Looking around, Pedro spotted his friend. Keeping his balance on the swaying deck, he hurried to help Jess.

"Get up!" he ordered. Jess groaned.

Pulling her up, Pedro dragged Jess across the deck.

They fell against the railing and caught their breath.

Suddenly, Jess looked around.

"Josh!" cried Jess. Panic was in her voice. "Where's my brother?"

Pedro shrugged. A big wave sloshed across the deck.

Jess shielded her eyes from the rain and looked up. Someone was in the crow's nest at the top of the main mast.

"Josh! Josh!" cried Jess, pointing up. She cupped her hands around her mouth and yelled louder.

He didn't hear her.

It was no use. The wind was too strong.

Pedro stood up. Together, they shouted again. This time, their voices rose above the wind.

Just then, Josh looked down. He waved his

arms in the air. Then he pointed below. The rope ladder to the crow's nest was gone. Josh had no way to get down.

Jess turned to Pedro. "Let's go," she said. Jess looped the rope around her shoulders.

Another wave hit the deck.

"Follow me," she cried, pulling Pedro's arm.

The rope ladder to mid-mast swung wildly in the wind. Jess reached for it and pulled herself up. Pedro was behind her.

"Hold on!" yelled Josh from above.

Jess was tossed back and forth as she climbed. The ladder was swinging in the wind. Higher and higher they went.

The ladder ended on the crossbeam at the middle of the mast. The crow's nest was just above.

Josh leaned over the crow's nest. But Jess was out of reach.

"Toss it!" yelled Josh, pointing to the rope on Jess's shoulder.

Jess nodded. Pedro held on to her.

Slowly, Jess freed her arms and made a loop with the rope. Around and around, she swung it in the air. Then she tossed it up.

Josh grabbed for the rope. He missed.

Jess tossed the rope again. On the second try, Josh caught the rope. He tied it to the crow's nest.

"Coming down!" yelled Josh, tugging on the rope.

Jess sighed with relief. She tied her end of the rope to the mast.

Jumping out of the crow's nest, Josh wrapped his feet around the rope and slid down.

Jess and Pedro grabbed Josh and pulled him in. He was shivering in his wet clothes.

"Are you okay?" cried Jess.

Slowly, Josh raised his head. He had a big grin on his face.

"Why are you laughing?" she scolded.

"That was fun!" said Josh. He glanced at Pedro, then at the deck below.

Both boys laughed.

"Whoopie!" yelled Pedro. "Race you down," he called and rushed to the riggings.

Josh got there first.

Jess stood by, shaking her head.

The sound of the boys' laughter rose above the wind.

"You're both crazy!" she yelled.

The rope ladder flapped back and forth. Carefully, Jess climbed down.

By morning, the sky was clear and the sea was calm again.

The storm was over.

Chapter 9
Mutiny?

The *Santa Maria* had been at sea for a month. The voyage was supposed to be three weeks. But no land was in sight.

The crew was tired and angry.

Jess and Josh were on deck with Uncle Harry. They sat around the fogón.

"Oh, man," said Josh. He looked at his bowl. Only hardtack and dried beans.

There was no hot meal today.

"One month at sea," growled the old seaman. The other sailors muttered under their breath.

"I'll not see my wife and sons again," said a young sailor.

"Aye," grumbled another man. "Never will I see my daughter's sweet face."

The crew was scared. Four weeks at sea was a long time.

A weary sailor turned to Uncle Harry. "How far have we gone, helmsman?"

Uncle Harry looked up. The sails were full. "The winds are at our back now," he said. "We are making good time."

"When will we see land?" asked the sailor.

"Soon," said their uncle.

"If we haven't reached the Indies," asked another seaman, "then where are we?"

The crew was afraid they were lost.

They blamed the captain.

On the poop deck, Columbus stood tall. Every day, he checked the compass and took measurements. Then he marked the logbook.

"I don't trust him," said Luis, nodding toward the captain. "He's not one of us." Columbus was from Italy, not Spain like the crew.

Luis grabbed some hardtack. He knocked the dried biscuit against the deck. Some weevils fell off. The bugs scurried away.

He stared at the biscuit in his hand.

Luis dunked the hardtack into a jar of stale water and ate it slowly. The men were tired of the bad food and long days at sea.

"Aye, will we run out of food and water, too?" asked the old seaman, shaking his head.

Jess ducked behind a crate. She turned on the Wizard and read:

o Wizard

In his journal, Columbus wrote: "Today the ships sailed 180 miles, but I recorded only 144 miles. I don't want the crew to worry if the voyage is too long."

Josh came over.

"Trouble," he said, looking back at the crew. "There might be a mutiny."

Jess nodded. "Columbus lied," she whispered. "We saw the logbooks."

"Yeah," said Josh. "*Two* of them."

"It's a trick," she said. "The men will find out about the false logbook if we don't see land soon."

The voices of the crew grew louder. Josh looked up.

Columbus climbed down from the upper deck. The men moved aside for the captain. They stood around him.

Everyone was quiet.

Columbus took a deep breath and smiled. "The air is sweet," he said. He leaned over the rail. "The sea is smooth," said the captain, waving his arm. "Land is ahead," he said. "I'm sure."

Luis stepped forward. "Are we lost, sir?" he asked bravely.

All eyes were on the captain.

"We're on the right course," said Columbus.

He clutched the logbook to his chest. "Trust me. It's all here."

He showed the false logbook to the men.

"Due west," said Columbus, pointing to the horizon. "We will reach the Indies in three days."

Just then, a loud shout came from the lookout above.

Pedro climbed the ropes to get a better look.

"Whale!" he yelled, waving wildly.

Everyone rushed to the railing.

"There," said Jess. Above the ocean rose a fountain of water.

A whale was blowing seawater out of its blowhole.

The sight of the whale cheered up the men.

They had hope.

Columbus had made a promise.

Three days until land.

Chapter 10
Land!

Josh leaned over the railing. Not a cloud was in the sky.

"Thirty-six days," said Jess. That was the last time that they had seen land.

"The Canary Islands are far behind us," said Pedro.

Jess looked into the bright sun. "I can't see *anything*!"

Josh gazed across the empty ocean. "Yeah," he said. "Just sea all around us."

Columbus had promised the crew. Land was ahead. But that was days ago.

Some sailors wanted to turn back to Spain.

They talked of mutiny. The crew might take over the ship.

Luis came over. "Have you heard the news?" he said. "There is a cash prize for the first man to sight land."

"A reward," asked Pedro, "for ship boys, too?" His eyes were wide with excitement.

"Aye, boy," said Luis, laughing. "You will be rich if you are the first to see land."

"Look," said Josh, pointing. Green weeds and small sticks floated in the water.

Luis nodded. Land was near.

By afternoon, flocks of birds were flying across the ship toward the southwest. There were gulls and terns. Sea birds *and* land birds.

Columbus shouted new orders. The ships turned southwest. The birds were leading them to land.

There was excitement on board.

The captain doubled the lookouts.

Late that night, the *Pinta* fired one of its guns.

"A cannon!" shouted Pedro from the crow's nest.

Everyone rushed on deck. The blast had come from the lead ship.

"Someone sighted land!" yelled Josh.

"Land ahoy!" cried Pedro in his loudest voice. "Land ahoy!"

The captain and the crew searched the open sea. But it was too dark to see.

It was a false call.

"Soon," said Columbus, looking toward the horizon. Dawn was near.

He turned and went below to check his charts.

It was October 12, 1492.

Jess sat on her blanket. The Wizard was in her lap.

> ○ wizard
>
> A lookout on the *Pinta*, Rodrigo de Triana, was the first to spot land. He saw a sandy beach in the moonlight, about six miles west. The ships were near the Bahama Islands, four hundred miles east of Florida.

"Show me," said Josh, sitting down beside Jess.

"Columbus never got to China," said Jess. "Just an island off the coast of North America."

"San Salvador," said Josh. "That's what he called the island."

"Columbus thought he had reached the Indies," said Jess.

"Big mistake," said Josh. He pulled his blanket over his head.

"He didn't find Asia," said Jess, putting away the Wizard. "But he did reach a New World."

At sunrise, the crew gathered on deck. They saw the coastline in the morning light.

The island was surrounded by dangerous reefs. The captain found an opening. He guided the *Santa Maria* and the two smaller ships into safe waters.

In the distance, the crew saw people on shore.

Columbus gave the order.

"Drop anchor!"

Luis and the others lowered small boats into the water.

Uncle Harry pulled Jess and Josh with him. Quickly, he leaped into the lead boat with Columbus.

"Hurry," he shouted.

Jess jumped first, and then Josh. Uncle Harry and Luis picked up the oars. Slowly, they rowed toward the shore.

Chapter 11

The New World

Up ahead was a long, white beach.

Jess and Josh clung to the sides of the small boat. Columbus sat in front.

"Look!" said Jess. Tall houses lined the beach. The huts were made of wooden poles covered with grass. Some people were running inside.

"They're scared," said Josh. He pointed to other people hiding behind trees.

The boats moved in closer.

Slowly, the native people came out of hiding and walked to the shore. Their eyes and skin were dark. Their long black hair was straight and thick. The men and women painted their faces and bodies with bright colors. Most did not wear clothes.

The captain was the first to jump onto land. The crew followed, carrying colorful banners of the king and queen of Spain. Josh and Jess carried the bags filled with gifts from Queen Isabella.

The colorful parade walked across the sandy beach.

Columbus stopped. He fell to his knees and wept with joy. He was sure that he had reached the Indies.

Watching was a group of amazed islanders.

"Why are they staring at us?" whispered Josh.

"They're surprised," explained Jess. "Maybe they've never seen fancy clothing."

"Yeah," said Josh, "or ships like ours."

The leader of the native people stepped forward. A parrot with bright red, yellow, and purple feathers was on his shoulder.

Columbus stood and unfolded a long paper. He held it up. A crest of castles and lions was at the top.

"That's it!" said Jess, pointing. It was the letter from the trunk in the attic.

Jess pulled Josh away from the crowd. No one noticed. All eyes were on the captain.

"I name this place San Salvador," read Columbus in a booming voice. "This land is the Indies. It now belongs to the king and queen of Spain."

The crew gave a cheer. The long voyage was finally over.

The island people looked at each other in surprise. They did not understand the words of this strange man.

Jess pulled out the Wizard, typed some words, and clicked:

When Columbus reached North America, he was greeted by the Taino people. He believed he had reached the Indies, so he called these native people "Indians."

"Another mistake," said Josh.

"Yeah," said Jess, "he thought that the Tainos were Asians!"

The voices around them got louder.

The islanders welcomed the strangers. They used their hands to speak. It was a celebration. The women and children brought baskets of food.

Everything was new to the crew.

"Pineapples," whispered Jess, "and corn, and sweet potatoes."

Josh took something from a basket. He handed it to Pedro.

"Try this," he said, grinning.

Pedro held the long red thing in his hand. He was curious, so he took a bite.

"Yikes!" cried Pedro, fanning his mouth. "It burns!" He ran to find some water.

Josh rolled over and laughed. *Hot peppers.*

"That wasn't nice," said Jess. She frowned at her brother.

Just then, Columbus shouted, "Bring the gifts!" The man with the parrot on his shoulder stood next to him. In his ears were gold earrings.

Jess and Josh dragged the bags to the front. The crew gathered around.

The captain opened the sacks. He handed

red woolen caps, colorful glass beads, and tiny tinkling bells to the islanders. The Taino leader raised his finger with the parrot. He placed the bird on Columbus's arm.

Then the man removed his gold earrings and put tiny bells in the holes. He handed the gold to Columbus. A trade.

The seamen leaned in closer. *"Gold,"* they murmured among themselves.

The leader pointed to the south. With his hands, he told Columbus about a large island. They called this place Cuba. The place to find more gold.

The crew was excited. *Was Cuba the Indian name for China?* they wondered.

"Not China," whispered Jess. "Cuba is near Florida."

Josh nodded. He remembered the island on the map in Uncle Harry's journal.

Suddenly, Jess felt a hand on her shoulder.

"Uncle Harry!" she said.

"Shh!" he said. He waved for them to follow.

Their uncle led Jess and Josh behind some trees, away from the crowd.

"It's time," said Uncle Harry. He pulled the time-compass from the leather bag.

"But the gold!" said Josh. He wanted to find treasure, too.

"Won't the crew miss us?" asked Jess.

"Maybe," said Uncle Harry. "They're taking six native people back to the ship. Some sailors are staying. I'll say you and Josh wanted to explore the island."

He cranked the hands to set the time-compass.

"Yeah," said Josh. "They'll forget about us."

Jess nodded.

"Gold," she said. "That's all they can think about."

Clicking sounds were coming from the time-compass. Uncle Harry was sending them back to the attic.

"Our mission is done," said their uncle. "With the queen's letter, Columbus made these lands in America a part of Spain."

"More people from Europe will come later," said Josh. "People from France, England, and Portugal — hundreds of explorers."

"Columbus really did discover a New World," said Jess.

"Awesome!" said Uncle Harry. Then he handed Jess his leather journal.

"Put it in the old trunk," he said.

Jess and Josh hugged their uncle.

The wind started to blow. The grass huts were spinning around them. The time-compass was working its magic.

Jess grabbed Josh's arm. She clutched the journal to her chest.

Faster and faster, the wind blew.

Uncle Harry faded away in a bright light.

Suddenly, everything was quiet.

Chapter 12
A Safe Place

It was midnight, about the same time as when they had left the attic.

Josh found the flashlight next to the old trunk. He turned the light on Jess. She was wearing her pink pajamas and bunny slippers.

"We're home," he said. Josh had on his pj's, too.

Slowly, Jess opened her eyes.

She handed Uncle Harry's journal to Josh.

"Let's check it," she said. Sometimes their uncle left clues about their next adventure.

"Nothing new," he said, flipping through the pages. "Just the map of Columbus's first voyage."

Josh shuffled over to the old trunk. He was sleepy.

"Wait!" said Jess, reaching in her pocket for the Wizard. She punched in some words and clicked Search. She read aloud:

---

o Wizard

October 12, 1492

Columbus returned to the *Santa Maria* that night with his native guides. Two days later, he set sail south in search of gold.

"Show me that map again," said Jess.

"Oh, brother," said Josh, yawning. Wasn't Jess tired, too?

He spread the journal on the lid of the trunk. It was open to the pages with the map.

"The flashlight," she ordered, walking over to the trunk.

"Okay, okay," said Josh. His sister was bossy.

He turned the beam of light on the Bahamas and islands to the south.

Jess clicked. Together, they read the next screen:

○ wizard

In his search for gold, Columbus sailed to Cuba, and later to the place we now call Haiti and the Dominican Republic. Except for a few bracelets on the natives, there was no gold.

"Just like the map shows," said Josh. He closed the journal and put it inside the trunk.

"And Columbus didn't find any treasure," said Jess.

She clicked to the next screen.

Her face went white.

"But he did find . . . dog-headed cannibals," said Jess in a quiet voice. "The natives told stories about monsters on the islands."

"That's silly," said Josh, closing the lid on the old trunk. "Those are just wild stories to frighten the sailors."

Jess read aloud from the next screen.

```
o wizard
```

On some islands, Columbus found fierce warriors. They covered their heads with parrot feathers and used paint to make horrible faces.

Jess shrugged. "I guess you're right. But the Tainos were friendly. They greeted the sailors with food and gifts."

She read some more. Finally, Jess put away the Wizard.

Josh led the way down.

"Eight months later," said Jess. "That's when Columbus returned to Spain. The queen made him a nobleman and gave him lots of money."

Just then, they heard sounds from below.

"Hurry," said Jess. "I hope Mom and Dad didn't hear us."

They tiptoed to the end of the hall. Josh stopped in front of his room.

Jess gave him a smile and ducked into her bedroom.

Her bed looked soft and warm.

And *safe*.

She jumped in and pulled the covers over her head.

Soon, she was fast asleep.